To Ava -

Rosie and the Wedding Day Rescue

Enjoy!

[signature]

For Hana,
my inspiration and Rosie look-alike.

Rosie and the Wedding Day Rescue

By
Lynelle Woolley

Illustrations by
Karen Wolcott

Flower Girl World: Rosie and the Wedding Day Rescue

Inquiries should be addressed to:
Markelle Media, LLC
12405 Venice Blvd., #350, Los Angeles, CA 90066
info@markellemedia.com

Library of Congress Control Number: 2011913907

ISBN: 978-0-9833116-3-8

Manufactured by Color House Graphics, Inc., Grand Rapids, MI, USA
August 2011
Job #35671
10 9 8 7 6 5 4 3 2 1

www.FlowerGirlWorld.com

Chapter One

"Rosie! Move!" Max cried out.

Max was trying to play a video game on the TV while his younger sister, Rosie, was inspecting the couch with a magnifying glass.

"Max, scoot over a little bit."

"ROSIE!"

"A-ha! Just as I suspected!" Rosie shouted. She reached between two cushions and pulled out a small, sparkling object. "I found Mom's earring!"

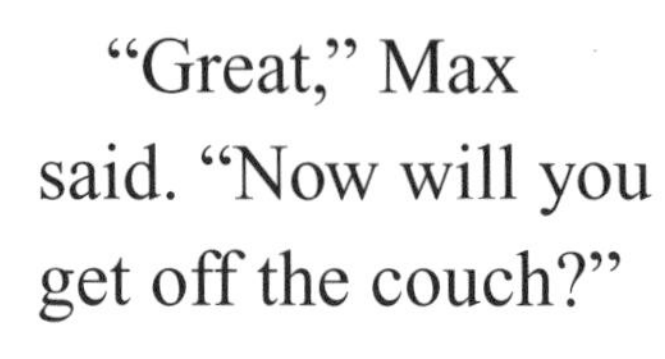

"Great," Max said. "Now will you get off the couch?"

Their mom rushed in from the kitchen. "Did I hear you found my earring? Where was it?"

"In the couch," Rosie said proudly, handing over the missing piece of jewelry. "You said the last time you wore it was Sunday. That was the day we all watched movies together. I figured this room was the best place to look."

"Rosie Anderson, you're an expert detective!" her mom said, giving her a huge hug.

Rosie beamed with delight. It was her dream to become a real detective and one day work for the FBI. She put her magnifying glass back into her special detective kit. It was a green tote bag filled with all sorts of gadgets, including binoculars, a flashlight, and fingerprint powder. Rosie carried her kit with her everywhere because a good detective is always prepared.

"Sweetie, I have something for you too," Mrs. Anderson said, giving Rosie an envelope made of delicate paper. Inside, Rosie found a card with a picture of a girl wearing a lavender dress. She was holding a basket overflowing with petals.

Rosie opened the card and read the inside. "It's from Greta. She's asking me to be a flower girl in her wedding."

Greta Goodwin was Rosie's favorite babysitter. She was a great hide-and-go-seek player; she made delicious ginger snap cookies; and she liked to climb trees as much as Rosie. Greta was a college student in Rosie's hometown of Washington D.C. Now she was graduating and marrying her boyfriend, Mark. Rosie wondered if she'd ever play hide-and-go-seek with her babysitter again.

"Why would Greta want me to be a flower girl?" Rosie asked. "I've never been one before."

"Being a flower girl is a very special honor," her mom replied. "Just because you haven't done it before doesn't mean that it won't be fun and exciting."

Rosie groaned. She really liked Greta, but she didn't like trying new things. There was always a chance that something could go wrong. She'd tried ballet once, but the tutu gave her a rash. Another time, she had tried a baking class and accidentally spilled cake batter all over herself *and* the cooking teacher! Rosie preferred to stick to the thing she loved best: detective work.

"Why do I have to try anything new?" Rosie asked. "My life is good the way it is."

"Rosie, trying new things is what life is all about," her mother replied. "Have you considered that Greta isn't even family, yet she likes you so much she wants you to be in her wedding?"

Rosie thought about her mother's comment. She didn't want to disappoint her favorite babysitter.

"Well...What would I have to do?" she asked.

"In a traditional wedding, the flower girl walks down the aisle right before the bride and throws petals on the ground. In a way, the flower girl announces the bride's arrival. That's a very important job, don't you think?"

Rosie liked the idea of being important. And throwing petals didn't seem so hard. Maybe she could do it for Greta's sake. Rosie tucked her light-brown hair behind her ears and announced, "Okay, I'll do it."

"Greta will be thrilled." Then her mother added, "When she gave me the card, we talked about all the details. She wants to meet in a couple of weeks to pick out the flower girl dress."

"HAH!" Max fell off the couch in a fit of laughter. "Rosie has to wear a dress?!"

Max knew his sister well. She was not a big fan of dresses. To be a detective, Rosie had to crawl on the ground and hide in all sorts of places. Those were not good activities for a dress.

"Max, stop laughing and get off the floor!" Mrs. Anderson said as she returned to the kitchen. "Rosie is going to be a beautiful flower girl. She only has to wear a dress for one day, and it will make Greta very happy."

Rosie felt dizzy. She fell back on the couch and covered her face with her hands.

"Oh, no," she thought. "What have I gotten myself into?"

Chapter Two

It was storming on the day that Rosie and her mom planned to meet Greta. When they arrived at the mall, the place was packed. Rosie remembered one other time when it had been this crowded. It was the day teen pop star Gaby Snow was there to sign autographs. As one of Gaby's biggest fans, Rosie waited in line for two hours to meet her, with no bathroom breaks!

Rosie wished she were seeing Gaby today instead of buying a dress. As she and her mom walked through the mall, Rosie dragged her rain boots as if they were filled with slushy mush.

"Think of it as detective work," her mom said, walking briskly. "You're on the search for the perfect flower girl dress."

Rosie scowled. Dress shopping was not detective work; it was torture!

"Rosie, we have to hurry. We don't want to keep the other flower girls waiting."

Rosie froze right in her tracks. "What?" she asked. "I didn't know there were other flower girls."

"Yes, there are two," her mom said, grabbing Rosie's hand to pull her along. "They are from out of town, and they're here today to help pick out the flower girl dress. Isn't that great?"

"What's so great about it?" Rosie said under her breath. She didn't like surprises. And now she was afraid there might be more.

"This must be it," said Mrs. Anderson, stopping in front of Bettina's Boutique.

Rosie's mouth dropped open. It looked like someone had set off a pink bomb inside the store. There were pink walls, pink decorations, pink carpet, and, of course, pink dresses everywhere. Rosie was planning her escape when a saleswoman with curly, carrot-colored hair approached them.

"Hello, ladies. I'm Bettina. How can I help you?" The saleswoman's voice squeaked with glee.

"We're meeting Greta Goodwin to pick out a flower girl dress," Rosie's mother replied, looking around the store for Greta.

"She isn't here yet, but this young lady is waiting for her too."

Bettina motioned across the room. Sitting in a lounge chair was a girl with big, brown eyes and two long, blond braids. In her lap Rosie could see a huge, fluffy purple ball of yarn. The girl was busy knitting.

Rosie's mom approached the girl, dragging Rosie behind her.

"Hello, I'm Mrs. Anderson, and this is my daughter, Rosie. Are you in Greta Goodwin's wedding too?"

"I'm Iris," the girl replied. "I'm one of Greta's flower girls. Greta is from Philadelphia, just like me. She was my babysitter before she went to college."

Mrs. Anderson grinned. "You and Rosie have a lot in common. What are you knitting? It's beautiful, don't you think, Rosie?"

Rosie knew her mom was trying to get her to talk to Iris. Instead of answering, she responded with a smile, the kind where the sides of the mouth go up and down really fast.

Iris didn't seem to notice. "Thanks," she said. "It's a scarf."

Iris got up to show off her knitting. Rosie wasn't interested in the scarf, but something else caught her eye.

Iris was wearing a T-shirt with sequins and a picture of Gaby Snow! "I like your shirt," Rosie blurted out.

"Thanks," said Iris, grinning. "I decorated it myself. My mom owns a flower and craft store, so we make stuff all the time."

"Where is your mom?" Mrs. Anderson asked.

"She's shopping somewhere in the mall." Iris looked at Rosie and rolled her eyes. "I guess there aren't enough shoe stores back in Philadelphia."

This made Rosie laugh. Her own mother was the exact same way about shopping.

Iris reached under the chair and pulled out a purple felt bag filled with beads, glue, scissors, and yarn. It reminded Rosie of her detective kit, which was hanging over her shoulder.

"I keep all my projects in my craft bag. Do you want to see the scrapbook I'm making for the wedding?" Iris asked.

"Sure," Rosie started to say. "I—"

But just then, a loud noise turned everyone's eyes to the front of the store.

"HI, Y'ALL! WE'RE HERE!"

Chapter Three

The greeting roared out like thunder from a dark-haired girl who was wearing a red top with a cheetah print skirt.

"Honey, don't shout!" said a woman with a Southern twang. She had very big, black hair.

Two little boys, who looked exactly alike, started running all over the store. Rosie watched as they ducked in and out of clothing racks, trying to tackle each other. Then one of them decided to use Bettina as a human shield.

"RICKY! RANDY! STOP IT AT ONCE!" This time, the roar came from the lady with the big hair.

The boys stopped immediately.

Bettina looked relieved. After smoothing out her dress, she cleared her throat and asked the woman, "How can I help you?"

"We're here to meet Greta Goodwin."

Rosie's mom stepped in. "That's why we're here too." She introduced herself, Rosie, and Iris.

"We're the Rubios," the girl piped up. "This is my mother, Regina, and these are my brothers, Ricky and Randy." She gave the boys a big-sister glare. "My name is Starrina Rubio, but I go by Starr Ruby. It's a fabulous stage name, don't you think?"

Rosie wasn't sure if Starr really expected an answer.

"We're from San Antonio, Texas," Starr went on. "Greta lived with us last summer.

She was supposed to be doing research at the university, but she took lots of breaks to play with me. I'm so excited to be in her wedding. I've never been a flower girl before, but as my daddy says, I was born to perform. I've been practicing my flower girl walk every day. Do you want to see?"

But before Starr could take a step, there were more shouts from the front of the store.

"Rosie! Starr! Iris!" It was Greta. Her blue eyes sparkled as she rushed over to the group. Rosie was the first to give the bride-to-be a big hug. For a moment, Rosie even forgot about being a flower girl.

After greeting everyone, Greta said, "I'd like you all to meet Amber. She's my second cousin and my maid of honor."

Greta motioned to a tall, thin young woman with straight, black hair. She was speaking into a red cell phone that had charms dangling from a chain – a shoe, a shopping bag, and a nail polish bottle.

Amber nodded to the group, and then quickly went back to her phone call. Mrs. Anderson and Mrs. Rubio wandered over to the lounge chairs to chat.

"What's a maid of honor?" Iris asked Greta.

"And what's a second cousin?" added Starr.

Rosie was glad they'd asked, because she didn't know either.

"Amber's mom and my mom are first cousins, so that makes Amber and me second cousins," answered Greta. "And a maid of honor is like the bride's special assistant. She helps the bride make decisions and get ready on the wedding day. She even holds the groom's ring until it's needed during the ceremony."

"But Ricky and Randy are the ring bearers. Isn't that their job?" Starr asked.

Greta smiled. "It's not that I don't trust them, Starr." She spoke softly so the boys wouldn't overhear. "But the twins are only six. I think it's better if they hold fake rings. Amber can be in charge of the real groom's ring. And Mark's best man will hold mine."

"I don't trust my brothers either!" Starr blurted out.

Rosie looked at Iris and Starr, and they all giggled together. The twins did seem very young and wild.

A second later, Amber finally ended her phone call. "Sorry," she said. "I had to cancel my nail appointment to come here today. It's been so hard to reschedule. What's happening?"

"I was just about to ask my flower girls which dresses they like," Greta said, looking around the store. "I want their recommendations so we can choose the perfect one. The flower girl dress is a very important part of the wedding." Then Greta turned to Rosie, Iris, and Starr. "So, girls, what do you think?"

Rosie's heart started doing flip-flops in her chest. "Uh-oh," she thought. "Now what do I do?"

Chapter Four

This was the moment Rosie had been dreading all morning. She didn't know the first thing about choosing a dress.

But Starr jumped right in. She proudly held up a dress with a zebra print top, a

leather belt, and a sparkly black skirt. "I love this one, don't y'all?"

Rosie thought it looked like something Gaby Snow would wear in a rock concert – not a flower girl dress. But she didn't say anything. She didn't want to hurt Starr's feelings.

"Hmmm..." Greta said as she examined it. "It's very unique, Starr." She glanced over at Iris. "What's your choice?"

Iris reached for a pink gown with flowers along the sash. "I like this one. The rosette appliqué is so cool."

"Rosette appliqué? What's that?" thought Rosie. She had no idea what Iris was talking about.

"That gown comes in a variety of colors," Bettina piped in.

"It's lovely," Greta said. Then she turned to Rosie. "Which dress do you like?"

"Uh…" Rosie's face turned red. Greta had said that the flower girl dress was an important part of the wedding. Rosie didn't want to ruin everything by picking the wrong one. Everyone was waiting, so she had to choose something.

Finally, Rosie pointed to the plainest dress in the store. It was white…and that was about it. "What do you think of this one?"

"It's nice," Greta responded. But Rosie saw her glance back at the dress that Iris had picked out.

"Amber." Greta turned to her cousin, who was back on the phone. "I need your help."

Amber put a hand over the speaker. "It's Nick. The only time he can confirm our weekend plans is now. He's such a busy boyfriend."

Greta sighed. "The girls each picked out a dress. Which one do you think would work best?"

Amber hadn't been paying attention. "Um…I like her choice." She pointed to Starr, who was closest to her. Then she went back to her call.

Starr beamed from ear to ear. Greta didn't seem as pleased. She faced the girls and said, "I think all three dresses are beautiful, but the one Iris chose will match the flowers at the ceremony. Let's go with that one."

Rosie's heart sank to the bottom of her rain boots. Her dress choice was a big failure. She had no idea why Greta had asked her to be in the wedding.

Bettina led the girls into the dressing room. She had each one try on an oversized sample gown. Iris and Starr didn't complain, but when it was Rosie's turn, she couldn't wait to get it off again. It was way too big and very uncomfortable. As Bettina pinned and poked her, Rosie looked at herself in the mirror. Besides the dress, she was wearing her rain boots and a big frown. She did not look like a perfect flower girl.

When Bettina finished fitting Rosie, she announced, "Girls, I want to welcome you to Flower Girl World."

"What's that?" asked Starr. Rosie and Iris were curious too.

"Flower Girl World is like a special club. Any young lady can join, but when you're in an actual wedding, you officially become a member."

This news made Rosie smile. Finally, there was something good about being a flower girl.

"How does it work?" asked Iris.

"As members, it's your duty to have fun at the wedding. Also, because you're sharing this special experience with each other, you must try to stay in touch in the future. And finally, the most important rule of all: You have to love everything about being a flower girl."

"Awesome!" exclaimed Starr and Iris together.

But Rosie said nothing. How could she be part of Flower Girl World if she didn't love everything about being a flower girl?

Rosie crossed her arms as she looked back in the mirror. "I don't think I can do this," she thought.

Chapter Five

"Honey, it's time to wake up. Today's the big day!" Mrs. Anderson said.

It was the morning of Greta's wedding, and Rosie was still in bed, buried under a huge pile of pillows. At first, Rosie didn't move. But then she let out an enormous cough that easily could have woken up the neighbors.

"I'm sick. I better stay in bed," Rosie said through her nose.

Her mom dug through the pillows to kiss her on the forehead.

"You don't feel hot to me. Maybe you should eat some breakfast." She pulled down Rosie's sheets and grabbed her hands to help her sit up. "You don't want to be late for the wedding, do you?"

It had been three months since the dress shopping trip, and Rosie wasn't feeling any better about being a flower girl.

"Do I really have to go?" Rosie said as she lay back down. Her nose no longer sounded

stuffed. "Greta has two other flower girls. I'm sure they can handle everything."

"Rosie, you made a commitment. Greta needs you. You have to go," her mother said firmly.

"What if I couldn't go? I mean, what if aliens landed in our backyard and took me to their planet? Then it would be impossible for me to be at the wedding."

"I'm sure that once the aliens found out you were a flower girl, they'd make an exception and bring you back." Rosie's mom pulled her up again. "Come on. I'm making chocolate-chip pancakes."

No one in Rosie's family could resist her mom's fluffy pancakes. Rosie knew her mother was trying to get her out of bed. And the plan worked.

After eating four pancakes, Rosie returned to her room and faced her closet. Her flower girl dress was still hanging in the plastic bag from the store. Rosie remembered how miserable she'd felt at the fitting. She dove back under her bed sheets.

"Rosie," Mrs. Anderson said. The young girl hadn't realized her mother was watching her through the doorway. "I'll help you put on the dress."

After zipping the back of the gown and tying the sash, Rosie's mom looked at her daughter. Her eyes filled up with tears. At first, Rosie thought her mom was angry with her for going back to bed, but then she noticed her mother was smiling too.

"Rosie, you look so pretty," her mom said. "You have to see yourself."

When Rosie turned toward the mirror, she was amazed at what she saw. Staring back at her was one of the most beautiful girls she had ever seen. The gown fit her perfectly, not like the uncomfortable sample dress.

“Iris made a good choice,” she said to her mom. “I mean, as far as dresses go.”

“Nice gown, Cinderella, but your hair could use a fairy godmother.”

Rosie turned around to see Max in the doorway. He had chocolate on his upper lip from the pancakes.

“And you need a shave,” Rosie replied, pointing to his sweet moustache.

Their mother cut in. “Rosie, you need to put on your shoes. We have to leave in fifteen minutes. Greta wants everyone in the wedding to be at the hotel early.”

Rosie looked back in the mirror as her mom and Max left the room. She turned from side to side to view herself from every angle. Nervous butterflies still fluttered inside her stomach, but finally, there were some excited butterflies in there, too.

Chapter Six

"Wow!" Rosie blurted out as she and her mom entered the breathtaking hotel lobby. A crystal chandelier sparkled above their heads. All around the room stood tall vases with sweet-smelling white flowers. Rosie wanted to sit on a puffy sofa, but her mom said no. Greta was waiting for them.

When they arrived at the suite, Rosie and her mom opened the door…and got a huge surprise. The place was a mess! Scattered everywhere were hair clips, brushes, bobby pins, hair spray, hangers, shoes, and lots of clothes. Greta and Amber were putting on makeup in one area; Iris and Starr were fixing their hair in another; and Ricky and Randy, dressed in tuxedos, were trying to do karate moves all over the place. Rosie thought everything looked wacky, except for one thing: in the far corner, gently hanging from a curtain rod, was Greta's wedding gown. It was covered in glistening pearls and delicate lace. Rosie couldn't wait to see Greta in it.

Everyone was too busy to notice that Rosie and her mom had arrived. "Hi, everyone!" Mrs. Anderson called out.

Greta turned from her mirror. "Hi!" The bride's voice cracked. "Thanks for dropping Rosie off early. I wanted all my wedding attendants here with me while I got ready for the ceremony. Now I think that was a crazy idea!" Greta laughed nervously before

taking in a big gulp of air. "I have to keep reminding myself to breathe."

At that moment, Amber's cell phone rang. She stood up to answer it, but Greta cut her off sharply. "Amber, no phone for now!"

"Fine," Amber replied, rolling her eyes. She went back to her makeup.

"Don't worry, Greta. Your wedding will be perfect," Mrs. Anderson said to the nervous bride. Then she turned to Rosie. "I have to go home to get ready. You're going to be perfect too." She gave her daughter a kiss before leaving the room.

Rosie didn't know what she was supposed to do next. She walked over to Starr and Iris and dropped her detective kit on the floor.

"Hi, Rosie," Iris said. "Greta asked us to wear these flower barrettes in our hair. Do you want me to help you with yours?"

"Me too," added Iris. "That's Gaby Snow. I love her."

Starr twirled around. "Did you see her on the cover of this month's *Kids Now* magazine?"

"I love that picture," said Iris.

"Me too," Rosie agreed.

Iris and Rosie picked up brushes and joined Starr. In their gowns, they looked like the best-dressed girl band ever.

"You're the one who makes things better. I hope that we're together forever."

"That would be great," Rosie replied. She sat down on a chair so Iris could reach the top of her head. "I'm not very good with fixing my hair. Brushing is about all I can do."

"I wish I didn't have to do anything to my rat's nest," Starr said, patting down her hair. "It takes a lot of work to get me ready for a big performance."

Rosie laughed out loud. Starr was so funny, and Iris was so nice. She could see why Greta liked them so much.

"Ahem." Starr cleared her throat. Then she began to sing into a hairbrush as if it were a microphone:

"Before I knew you, who was I? You're the one who changed my life."

"Hey, I know that song," Rosie said.

Starr's twin brothers cheered like fans at a rock concert as the three girls kept singing.

"When times are tough, you're always there.

I know I don't have to be scared.

We'll be together until the end. Why?

YOU'RE MY BEST FRIEND!!!

Woo, yeah. YOU'RE MY BEST FRIEND."

The girls were really rocking out. Ricky and Randy started crazy-dancing. They bumped into a table, scattering hair clips all over the floor – things were getting out of control. That's when Greta swung around in her chair and screamed, "CUT IT OUT!!"

Her roar was as loud as a firecracker. It surprised everyone, so much so that Randy lost his balance and slid into Ricky, and Ricky went flying...right in the direction of Greta's bridal gown! Everyone gasped, but only Greta could get a word out.

"NOOOOOOOOO!!" she screeched as she flew out of her chair. But she was too late. To break his fall, Ricky grabbed on to Greta's dress and ripped a big hole in the lace!

The room went silent. After a few seconds, Ricky pointed to Randy and wailed, "It's his fault!"

"You tore the dress, not me," Randy squawked, heading toward his brother with both fists clenched.

"Stop it!" Starr was angry. "You're both to blame. You wrecked Greta's wedding." She dragged them away from the dress so she could yell at them some more.

Rosie stood frozen. She didn't know what to do. The wedding was supposed to start in one hour. But now Greta's dress was ruined. Greta sobbed while Amber tried to calm her down.

"Those boys are rodents," Amber said. "And now you've messed up your makeup too!"

Amber seemed to be making things worse. Rosie wished she could help Greta feel better, but she didn't know what to say. How could a kid help a grown-up?

"It doesn't look too bad."

Everyone turned in the direction of the voice. It was Iris. She was examining the dress closely.

"I think I can stitch it up and no one will even notice. Let me see if I have ivory thread."

"Iris?" Greta was able to get some words out between sobs. "Do you really think you can fix it?"

"No problem!" Iris said, holding up a spool from her craft kit.

Iris sat down on the couch with the torn dress and went to work. Rosie was amazed. Iris was saving the day. "I wish I could help Greta too," Rosie thought.

"All done," Iris said a short while later. She tried to stand up with the dress, but it was too big and heavy.

"I can't thank you enough," said Greta, taking the gown from Iris and giving her a hug.

Amber grabbed Greta's arm and led her to the dressing area. "You have to hurry. The wedding starts in a half hour!"

Rosie looked at the clock. Amber was right. Soon they would all be walking down the aisle!

Chapter Seven

Rosie, Starr, and Iris couldn't wait any longer. While Greta finished dressing, they snuck downstairs to peek inside the magnificent grand ballroom.

Through the open door, they could see a long, red carpet aisle that led to a tall arch covered with white roses and lilies. Guests in tuxedos and elegant ball gowns were mingling. Everyone seemed to be having a great time, and the wedding hadn't even started yet.

"I'm nervous," Iris said as they hurried back upstairs. "There are so many people in there."

Rosie agreed. "There are probably a million guests."

"Don't worry," said Starr. "If you get scared, do what I always do: picture the audience as pigs. It works every time. And from the looks of that room, we're going to be staring at some very fancy pigs."

All three girls were oinking and laughing when they walked back into the bridal room and saw the most beautiful sight: Greta in her wedding gown. She looked like a princess in a royal wedding. Greta's smile was gleaming, just like the pearls on her dress.

"You're so pretty," Rosie said to Greta.

"Yes, she is," Amber replied, looking at herself in the mirror, not at Greta.

"Thank you," the bride said to Rosie. "It's time to get started. Is everyone ready?" Greta took a deep breath. "Ring bearers, do you have your ring pillows?"

"Yes!" Ricky and Randy shouted.

"Flower girls, do you have your baskets?"

"Yes!" Rosie, Iris, and Starr cheered.

"Amber, do you have the groom's ring?"

"What are you talking about?" Amber replied, turning from the mirror, looking confused.

Greta gave her a confused look back.

"What do you mean? I gave you the ring to hold during the ceremony."

Amber's cheeks turned the color of her pink dress. She paused and then looked directly at the twins.

"I thought the ring bearers were supposed to hold the bride's and groom's rings. I gave Mark's to one of them. I don't know which one; I can't tell them apart."

"I don't have the groom's ring," Randy piped up.

"Neither do I. We have fake rings on our pillows. See?" Ricky held up his cushion.

"You didn't give us the real ring. You're lying!" Randy shrieked at Amber.

"You two sewer rats are such trouble-makers. You probably lost the ring when you were scurrying around the room." Amber turned to Greta. "I'm so sorry they're causing more problems for your wedding."

The boys were furious. They yelled at Amber, and she yelled back. Their screaming grew louder and louder. Finally, Greta hollered, "ENOUGH!!!"

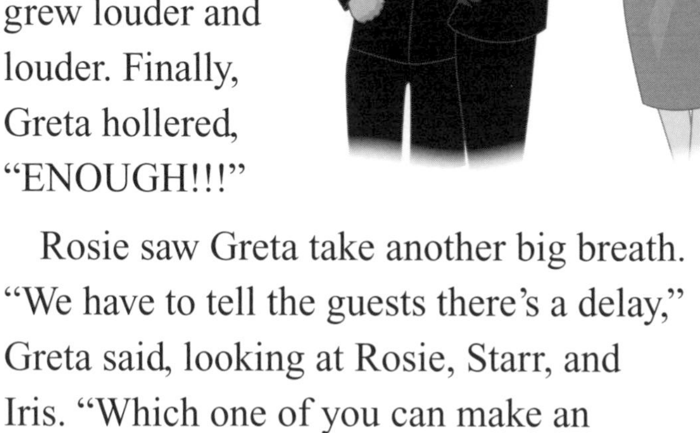

Rosie saw Greta take another big breath. "We have to tell the guests there's a delay," Greta said, looking at Rosie, Starr, and Iris. "Which one of you can make an announcement?"

Rosie gulped. She didn't want to disappoint Greta, but she was nervous about speaking in front of such a big crowd. Even if the room was full of pigs!

"I'll do it," Starr cried, jumping up and down.

"Rosie and Iris, please go with her. As soon as you've made the announcement, come back here. Amber, the twins, and I will start searching the room for Mark's ring, but we'll need your help."

"Should we ask others to help too?" Iris asked.

"No." Greta shook her head. "Having more people in the room will make it harder to search. Let the guests know everything is okay and that we hope the delay will be short."

Rosie, Starr, and Iris bounded out the door and down the staircase.

"What will you say?" asked Iris, panting as they ran.

"I don't know, but I'll think of something," answered Starr.

Rosie had no doubt about that.

The girls rushed through the ballroom door and headed toward the front. The guests stopped their conversations, surprised to see the flower girls by themselves.

Starr grabbed the microphone. "Hello, everyone! Welcome to the wedding." She paused for dramatic effect. "I'm sorry, but we have a little problem."

Everyone gasped.

"Don't worry," Starr added quickly. "We have to start the ceremony a little late, that's all. It's no big deal." She grinned. "We know you want to

see us flower girls drop our petals. You'll just have to wait a little longer."

The guests laughed and clapped loudly. As the girls hurried back down the aisle, Rosie realized something: "Now I'm the only flower girl who hasn't helped the bride." But there was no time to worry about that. The flower girls had to get back to the bridal suite to search for the missing ring!

Racing up the stairs, Starr said, "Are either of you good at finding small objects?"

For the first time since she was asked to be a flower girl, a confident smile spread across Rosie's face.

Chapter Eight

When the girls returned to the bridal suite, Amber and the twins were still yelling at each other. Greta was crawling around on her hands and knees in her wedding dress, looking for the ring underneath furniture.

"Things don't look good in here," Starr said.

"You're right," Iris agreed. "Finding that ring is going to be impossible."

"Maybe not," Rosie chimed in. "I know what to do."

Before her new friends could ask what she meant, Rosie started calling out instructions.

"Starr, you focus on your brothers. Find out if they know anything about the ring."

"Okay," Starr replied.

"Iris, can you take care of Greta? She

shouldn't be crawling on the floor. She's going to ruin her dress."

"Sure," Iris said. She lowered her voice. "I'll keep Amber away from her, too."

"What are you going to do, Rosie?" Starr asked.

"I'm going to find the ring! Luckily, I have all my detective tools with me," Rosie said, holding up her detective kit.

"Cool!" The other girls were impressed.

"But we have to hurry," Rosie added. "The wedding guests are waiting!"

Starr yanked her brothers away from Amber. They were like tigers ready to pounce on the maid of honor.

Iris kneeled on the floor next to Greta. She put an arm around the bride and led her over to the couch. "Rosie will find the ring, Greta. Don't worry."

Rosie dug through her kit. "Hmmm..." she thought. "What's the right tool for a situation like this?" It really wasn't the time for fingerprint powder.

Suddenly, there was a knock on the door. Amber jumped out of her chair to answer it, but Greta stopped her. "Amber, no one enters this room, and no one leaves until the ring is found!" she said fiercely.

"But...But..." Amber said. "I just thought—"

"Please don't think anymore," Greta cut her off. "You've already caused enough trouble."

Amber sunk back into her chair.

The knocking finally stopped. By then, Rosie had found the perfect detective tool: binoculars! She would use them to scan the room for anything unusual. But before she could begin her search, Starr came over to report on her conversation with her brothers.

"I think the boys are telling the truth. I know when they're lying, and this isn't one of those times. Something fishy is going on."

"I agree," Rosie said, raising the binoculars to her eyes and peering all over the room.

Just then Amber's cell phone started ringing. "Oh great, it's Nick!" she said, reaching for the red phone.

"Don't you dare answer that," Greta snapped.

"Fine," Amber said in a huff. She dangled the phone by its charm chain. "Then I suppose you should take it away from me."

Rosie continued scanning the room

until her eyes came to rest on Amber.

"Greta!" Rosie burst out a second later. "I found the ring!"

Chapter Nine

Greta leaped to her feet. "What? Where is it?" She wiped tears from her eyes.

Rosie walked over to Amber and took the cell phone out of her hand. Hanging from her charm chain were tiny figures of a shoe, a shopping bag, a nail polish bottle—and the groom's ring! Rosie gave the ring to Greta.

"Now I remember!" exclaimed Amber. "I was afraid I'd forget where I put the ring. Nick suggested that I attach it to my cell phone. He knows how much I love my cell phone."

Amber laughed. But realizing that no one else thought it was funny, she stopped.

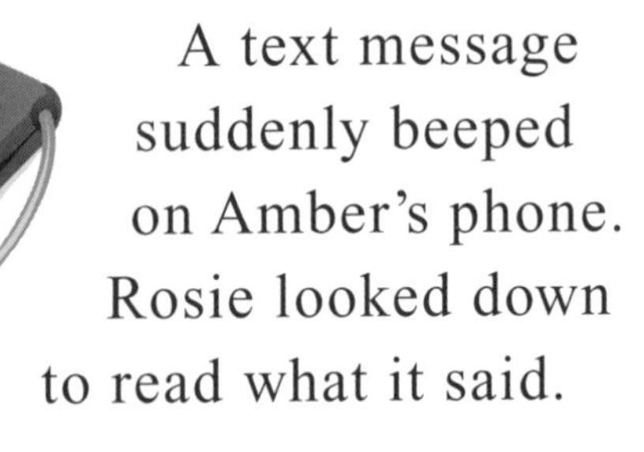

A text message suddenly beeped on Amber's phone. Rosie looked down to read what it said.

Knocked. No answer. Ring on cell phone.

Amber grabbed the phone from Rosie.

"It's from Nick. He must have figured out why the wedding was delayed," she went on. "The mystery is solved. Now it's time for all of us to walk down the aisle."

"I don't think you'll be walking down the aisle, Amber," Greta said, holding the ring tightly.

Amber looked confused.

"A maid of honor is supposed to *help* the bride, not cause problems for her. You care more about your cell phone and your boyfriend than this wedding. Our moms wanted you to be my maid of honor, but let's face it: we've never been very close."

Amber's eyes opened wide. "What? What am I supposed to do?"

"You can join Nick in the audience, if you like."

Amber's face turned bright red. "I'm sorry that things didn't work out." She grabbed her bag and scurried out the door without saying goodbye.

Rosie supposed that Amber wouldn't be in the audience, but now was the time to focus on happier thoughts. Greta had the ring back, and Rosie was the one who found it. "I guess I'm a good flower girl after all!" she thought to herself.

Greta glanced in the mirror and wiped the makeup smudges off her face. Then she turned to the girls. "I don't know what I would have done without you three. Thank you so much. Rosie, you saved the wedding by finding Mark's ring."

Rosie beamed. "It wasn't just me," she said, grabbing the hands of her two friends.

"You're right," Greta said. "Now I have a special request: Will you three be my flower girls of honor?"

Rosie, Iris, and Starr gathered around Greta and gave her a huge, happy hug. They didn't need to say anything. Greta had her answer.

Chapter Ten

Rosie's heart was thumping so hard she thought she might fall down. She, Iris, and Starr stood outside the ballroom, waiting for their turn to walk down the aisle. Rosie was nervous, but more than anything, she was excited. Greta had given her an important job: she was in charge of the groom's ring!

"That's our cue," Iris said as the music changed to an upbeat tune. She glanced back at her friends. "Good luck!" she said before heading down the aisle.

After a few beats, Starr followed her. Finally it was Rosie's turn. She wondered if she'd be able to move her legs, because they were shaking like crazy. All it took was one scary first step…and then she was fine.

Rosie gently tossed her petals to the ground. She looked out into the audience and tried to imagine the guests as pigs. It didn't work until she spotted Max. Seeing him as an oinker with a tie was so funny, she almost burst out laughing. But then she remembered her important job and shifted her focus back to the petals.

When Rosie reached the end of the aisle, the music switched to *Here Comes the Bride*. All the guests stood, hoping to get a good view of Greta. As the bride came through the door, Rosie glanced over at Mark, who was standing on the other side of the arch. She could tell he had tears in his eyes, but his smile stretched from ear to ear.

During the ceremony, Rosie focused her attention on the justice of the peace, who was in charge of marrying Greta and Mark. She listened anxiously for him to say six important words:

"May I please have the rings?"

Rosie took the groom's ring off her thumb and proudly presented it. Then she waited for six more important words.

"You may now kiss the bride."

As the couple kissed, everyone clapped. Now it was time to celebrate!

The party room down the hall overflowed with enormous flower arrangements. Waiters passed trays of bite-sized food and glasses of bright red punch. A big band played slow songs and loud rock 'n' roll. Rosie, Iris, and Starr never left the dance floor…except when the wedding cake was served.

While eating her slice of cake, Rosie was filled with joy. Being a flower girl was so much better than she'd ever imagined. "I'm glad I tried it," she thought. But then she realized that the wedding would soon be over.

“I wish we lived in the same city,” she said to her new friends. “Then we could play all the time.

Iris looked sad. “Maybe we’ll be in a wedding together again someday,” she said.

“Probably not,” Starr said. “We don’t know the same people, except for Greta and Mark.”

"Hey!" Rosie remembered something important. "Didn't Bettina say that we're official members of Flower Girl World?"

"That's right!" Iris agreed. "She also said that we should try to keep in touch after the wedding."

Rosie added, "We can email each other and send pictures, and help each other if we're ever flower girls again!"

For once Starr was quiet. Rosie noticed she looked upset. "What's wrong, Starr?" she asked.

"I just thought of something," said Starr. "You both have flower names. 'Rosie' and 'Iris' are perfect for Flower Girl World. But what about me?"

"I know! You can be a stargazer lily!" Iris replied. "It's one of my favorite flowers in my mom's shop. It's pretty and pink, but you have to be careful. It will stain your clothes."

"That does sound like me." Starr was smiling. "I always like to leave a lasting impression."

"That's for sure!" her new friends agreed.

"There's one more thing we have to do," Starr said.

She hurried over to the bandleader and whispered in his ear. Rosie couldn't hear because of all the noise, but she knew her friend was up to something. Then Starr motioned for Rosie and Iris to join her. As they climbed up onto the stage, Starr grabbed the microphone.

"Ladies and gentlemen, we want to toast the bride and groom. Congratulations!"

Around the large room, glasses clinked.

"And now we'll sing them a special song." She turned to the bandleader. "Please cue the music."

Rosie and Iris looked at each other nervously. What was Starr about to make them do? A guitar began to play, and when the piano and drums joined in, they knew exactly what was going on. They picked up microphones, ready to put on a show.

"Before I knew you, who was I?

You're the one who changed my life.

You're the one who makes things better.

I hope that we're together forever.

When times are tough, you're always there.

I know I don't have to be scared.

We'll be together until the end. Why?

YOU'RE MY BEST FRIEND!!!

Woo, yeah. YOU'RE MY BEST FRIEND."

The guests jumped out of their seats, clapping wildly. The girls were like pop stars!

"Thank you! We're called Flower Girl World," yelled Starr above the crowd. Then she added, "Book us for your next wedding!"

Everyone cheered. The three girls hugged. It was the start of a great adventure in friendship.

COMING SOON!

MORE FLOWER GIRL WORLD CHAPTER BOOKS

Learn more about all our books at
www.FlowerGirlWorld.com/books

Iris and the Aloha Wedding Adventure

Starr and the High Seas Wedding Drama

PICK UP OUR FIRST PICTURE BOOK!

Camellia the Fabulous Flower Girl

Join Camellia and her new friends Poppy and Willow for a fabulous and fun trip down the aisle.

JOIN US IN FLOWER GIRL WORLD

for a Magical and Memorable Experience!

FUN FOR YOU

Games, activities, crafts, and more.

FLOWER GIRL ADVICE

We'll help guide you down the aisle.

GREAT ADVENTURES

Discover more stories featuring the Flower Girl World characters. There are so many different wedding customs and locations to explore.

www.FlowerGirlWorld.com

FLOWER GIRL WORLD™